BOOKS BY KEN SCHOLES

<u>*The Psalms of Isaac*</u>
Lamentation
Canticle
Antiphon
Requiem
Hymn

Metatropolis: The Wings We Dare Aspire
(with Jay Lake)

<u>*Novella*</u>
Last Flight of the Goddess

<u>*Collections*</u>
Long Walks, Last Flights and Other Strange Journeys
Diving Mimes, Weeping Czars & Other Unusual Suspects
Blue Yonders, Grateful Pies and Other Fanciful Feasts

IF DRAGON'S MASS EVE BE COLD AND CLEAR

FOR BRIAN —
HO, HO, HO!

IF DRAGON'S MASS EVE BE COLD AND CLEAR

KEN SCHOLES

FAIRWOOD PRESS
Bonney Lake, WA

IF DRAGON'S MASS EVE BE COLD AND CLEAR
A Fairwood Press Book
Copyright © 2011
by Kenneth G. Scholes

All Rights Reserved

No part of this book may be reproduced or transmitted
in any form or by any means, electronic or mechanical,
including photocopying, recording, or by any
information storage and retrieval system, without
permission in writing from the publisher.

Fairwood Press
21528 104th Street Ct E
Bonney Lake WA 98391

See all our titles at:
www.fairwoodpress.com

"If Dragon's Mass Eve Be Cold and Clear"
originally appeared at *Tor.com* © 2011
and was reprinted in *Blue Yonders, Grateful Pies
and Other Fanciful Feasts* © 2015

"The Doom of Love in Small Spaces"
originally appeared in *Realms of Fantasy* © 2008
and was reprinted in *Long Walks, Last Flights
and Other Strange Journeys* © 2008

ISBN: 978-1-933846-86-6

Fairwood Press First Edition:
November 2019

Cover image © 2019 by Orion Swenson
Cover and book design by Patrick Swenson

Printed in the United States of America

*For Amber,
Who's Teaching Me Now
From Another Angle*

CONTENTS

Preface   10
by Tina Connolly

If Dragon's Mass Eve   13
Be Cold and Clear

BONUS TRACK
The Doom of Love   81
in Small Spaces

Afterword &   114
Acknowledgement

PREFACE
by
Tina Connolly

The Santaman came reeking of love into this place and we did not know him.

THE FIRST TIME I ENCOUNTERED THIS story, I was struck by the gorgeous mix of strange and familiar presented right there in the opening. Not Santa, but *The Santaman*. Poetry and faith and world-strands and ash and here is the Santaman, *reeking* of love.

I love stories that deal with the intersection of myth and faith and reality. I love stories that feel like they are just a small piece of a fantastical whole; that there is a massive iceberg of worldbuilding, just out of sight. There are a million beautiful details in Ken's piece that speak to a world we can half imagine, half comprehend; a world set just around the corner from ours. We don't know if that corner is a step into the future, or a sidle into an alternate world. We don't need to. We see father and daughter preparing their red paper hats with the cotton ball, and we understand that they are carrying out very old, very familiar traditions.

I buried my father on Dragon's Mass Eve.

The second time I encountered this story, it was to help bring it to life in a different way. Marshal Latham from the podcast "Journey Into..." asked me to narrate Mel Farrelly's story, as part of a larger, full cast recording. I jumped at the chance immediately. As an actor, some characters just speak to you. You know exactly how you want to inhabit them, how to help them say what they want to say. Mel is dealing with grief and holidays and moving forward into life again. She is the guardian for an absent hope mine. Hope is powdery and flaky, bitter and sweet. Hope has been absent for a very long time.

No one really believed in the Santaman until he came with his tattered red robe and his dripping red sword.

When the hope mine is dead, how do you believe that hope will be found once more? When the Dragon's Mass Eves continue to be cold and clear, how do you believe that the Santaman will ever return? Being right, says Mel's father, is not always required.

This is his story. This is our story, too.

There are common themes in Ken's work. Of love and faith and a world full of half-understood legends; beliefs dissolving around you. Of people, plunging forward, trying to do the right thing. Of trying to find a way forward, even if we don't really know if the Santaman will ever come again, and we aren't quite sure we believe. Of finding hope, where all was lost. *If Dragon's Mass Eve Be Cold And Clear* deals with all of these. It is strange and wondrous and compassionate and gorgeous, and I hope you love it, too.

IF
DRAGON'S
MASS
EVE BE
COLD
AND
CLEAR

Muscles tire. Words fail. Faith fades. Fear falls. In the Sixteenth Year of the Sixteen Princes the world came to an end when the dragon's back gave out. Poetry died first followed by faith. One by one the world-strands burst and bled until ash snowed down as huddled masses whimpered in the cold.

The Santaman came reeking of love into this place and we did not know him.

This is his story.

This is our story, too.

—Prelude
The Santaman Cycle,
Authorized Standard Version
Verity Press, 2453 YD

I buried my father on Dragon's Mass Eve. I dug the grave myself, there on the hill overlooking our homestead, beside the grave he dug for my mother some thirty-five years earlier.

As I worked the shovel, I tried not to cry. I failed. And I recited the Cycle, just the way he taught me, as I cut the sod and turned the dirt out into a pile.

Muscles tire. It was as if he stood with me. I could hear his voice grumbling on the wind that rose as the sun dropped and the air cooled. "Pause, Melody Constance," he said. "Feel what the writer intended with the words."

I felt my foot upon the shovel, my shoulders as I bent and lifted dirt. I felt the hollow empty place inside that tried to swallow me whenever my eyes wandered to the wagon and the red-wrapped body laying there.

Words fail. Again, a hesitation, a waiting. Silence to honor the moments no words can carry.

Like this one.

Only, it didn't feel like a moment—it felt like a year, in the cold, working the shovel. Alone. Orphanhood settled onto my back and shoulders with a weight I'd never felt before. I had no memory of my mother; she'd died the morning I was born. So it was a loss I assumed and grew into, never really knowing what I'd missed out on other than those times I stayed with neighboring families when my father needed to travel. But even then, it was only the slightest taste of someone else's life. Working the mine and farm with my father was *my* life. And so was Dragon's Mass Eve—his favorite and only holiday— spent quietly at home in our red paper hats and our fruit salad and rice stew while the faithful gathered at church.

Faith fades. Fear falls.

My mind blurred with my eyes as the tears overpowered me. The questions began to rise even as the fear fell upon me. What will I do now? Where will I go? How will I ever learn to live around this vast hole in my heart?

They were all things we'd talked about in passing when he talked in the midst of his illness about not getting better. And I knew that I would find the desk in his office perfectly organized with carefully written instructions for everything that needed to be done and everyone that had to be contacted. He'd learned to be meticulous during forty years working in the Bureaucracy's supply chain, and he'd instilled it into me. I think I was six when he put the first of many carefully scripted lists into my hands and sent me off to do my chores.

But having a plan and executing said plan were not the same thing.

My eye wandered to the wagon again, and I tried to tell myself it was because I was measuring how much further I had to dig. But I knew better. It was because I was close to finished. And when I was done digging, when I eased my father into that hole, he would be gone. I would only ever see him again in memory and dreams, in the half-dozen photographs tucked into our leatherbound copy of the Cycle.

This would be our last Dragon's Mass Eve together. My last time reciting the words with him. Our conversation earlier that morning would be the last we ever had, and it broke my heart open even further.

I went through the Cycle three times before I finished digging, from *muscles tire* to *upon his back, a world*, quoting from the Authorized Standard Version that my father had studied during the single year he spent in seminary. It was the version he'd memorized as a part of his training, and though he'd set aside his faith years before, he still felt it had enough merit that his daughter should know it. So now I said the words, felt none of them, and gentled my father into his grave.

The night was clear and cold but I paid it no mind. The hymn might've promised that the Santaman's grace would find us here, but the reality was I'd already seen at least a half-dozen clear and cold Dragon's Mass Eves, and the Santaman had yet to come back, reeking of anything, much less love. There had been, according to my father, over two hundred and thirty seven cold, clear Dragon's Mass Eves to be exact, much to the great consternation of the few remaining theologians.

We were on our own.

I was on *my* own.

I shoveled the earth over him and went through the Cycle another three times for good measure. But even as I did, I knew it wouldn't be enough. It was my first lesson in grief—that there never, ever was enough when it came to those we lost.

On my last Dragon's Mass Eve with Father, the rice stew grew cold upon the stove and I did not kneel and pray to the north. Instead, I cried myself to sleep, still covered in the dirt and drying sweat of my father's grave-digging.

> *If Dragon's Mass Eve be cold and clear*
> *The Santaman's grace may find us here.*
> *But if Dragon's Mass Eve be clouded sky*
> *The Santaman's grace may pass us by.*
>
>   —Hymn #475,
>   "If Dragon's Mass Eve Be Cold
>   and Clear"
>   *Hymns of the Dragon and his Avenger,*
>   Contemporary Edition
>   Verity Music, 2623 YD

"LIKE THIS," MY FATHER TOLD ME, unfolding the red paper and then folding it again in a different place, pressing the new crease into it with his massive thumb.

I watched, then took it from him and folded it again. It was my tenth Dragon's Mass Eve and it had gone like all of the others I could remember. First, he pulled out the jars and cans he'd collected over the year, separating the fruit from the vegetables and the cans of potted meat. The fruit came to me along with a notation on my morning chores list, and I mixed it into a fruit salad. His own list called for preparing the rice stew, and while it simmered, we moved on to the hats.

"I can never get it right," I said.

He chuckled, and it was a low rumble in the brightly lit kitchen. "Getting it right isn't always required."

I watched his hands as they moved over his own sheet of paper, a fold here and a fold there, followed by a dab of paste and a cotton ball. I looked at mine and sighed. "Yours is better."

Lifting the hat, he placed it on my head and then pushed up his glasses. Then, he swept my paper and cottonball away with a giant hand and started over with them. "Mine is a wreck," he said with a toothy grin. He nodded to the hat I wore. "Yours looks pretty good, actually."

We laughed, and after, he put the battered hat onto his head. "Now," he said, "we are ready."

We stood and went outside into the night. We climbed the hill out behind the homestead and faced north, kneeling at my mother's grave. The stone that marked it was plain, dark granite.

Harmony Angelique Sheffleton-Farrelly, it read. Then, after the date of her birth and the date of her death: *Public servant, beloved wife and mother.*

My knees were cold. "I don't understand why we do this," I said. Ten was the year that I mastered the art of the subtle complaint.

"We do this," he said, "because it's important to remember where we come from."

Of course, I'd heard the story of how he and Mother had met and about their first Dragon's Mass Eve together in the supply basement of the Bureaucracy. He'd been one of a small number of trolls in public service to the Bureaucracy, his trollishness coming in handy for safeguarding their supplies. My mother had been his replacement after thirty years in the supply chain, but meeting her had caught some part of him on fire and he'd decided to forego retirement. They spent another decade improving efficiencies, easing the government back to some semblance of functional. Then they'd ridden west with some of the world's last hope lining the bottom of an old coffee can to seed a mine that had long before gone dry. They raised a litter of love, selling off each pup that survived, and made due on their pensions.

Somewhere in the midst of it, they decided to have me, and that choice changed everything.

I put my hand on the stone. "But we don't believe in the Santaman," I said.

"No," he said and winked. "We don't have to."

We said our prayer quickly as the wind rose to threaten our hats. When we finished, I looked up. "Clouded sky," I said.

Father chuckled again. "Yes."

"Last year was clear, though."

"Yes," he said again. "There have been quite a few clear, cold Dragon's Mass Eves."

I kicked the dirt. "The song got it wrong."

I felt his hand settle onto my shoulder. "Getting it right," he said again, "isn't required." We went back into the house and

I pulled the door closed. He went to the stove and ladled the rice stew into simple wooden bowls that came out each year just for this tradition. He didn't speak again until we were seated at the table, the fire crackling nearby.

"Besides," he said as he tucked his napkin into his open-collared shirt, "they changed the song a long time ago. While I was in seminary there were a lot of people wanting to update the Cycle and the Hymnal. The song used to say 'will,' which implied a guaranty that the clergy couldn't afford to underwrite once the cold, clear nights started showing up again."

I'd heard this one before and I nodded. "So they changed it to 'may.'"

He grinned, his broad face lighting up. "Yes."

I tried to imitate his deep, gruff voice. "So when we sing it, we sing it as it was written—"

He joined in and we finished in unison. "—just as the writer intended it to be sung."

If Dragon's Mass Eve Be Cold and Clear   27

I paused, my spoon paused above the rim of the bowl. "But it isn't true."

He paused, too. "No, it doesn't appear to be."

"So aren't the new words more . . . accurate?"

He took a bite, swallowed, and thought for a moment. "Only if the underlying premise is accurate. I can sing about flying fish that *might* bring little girls vast wealth for Dragon's Mass Eve, but if there *are* no flying fish . . ." Here, he shrugged.

I smiled and mimicked his shrug. "And so we return to my initial question. Why do we do it?"

My father sighed. "Someday, when you have a child, you'll understand it better, I think."

I shook my head. "I don't think I will." Then, I wrinkled my nose. "And I don't want a child."

"Ah," he said, "but do you want your present?"

I nodded. "But let me get yours first."

That was the year that I'd written him

a story about the two of us fighting Black Drawlers in the north while we searched for the Santaman's fabled sword. I'd written it out in my best penmanship, and Miss Marplesbee, the sole teacher at the small one-room school in town, helped me bind it between pieces of cardboard with bright red yarn. I was particularly pleased with the cover—one of my better drawings of Father lopping the head off a Black Drawler with me poised carefully on his back, a dagger clenched in my teeth.

And it was the year that he gave me the picture of Mother, wearing the dress she wore when she met my father, leaning against a desk in the drab cubicle wasteland of the Bureaucracy's fifth floor. He'd built the frame himself.

I was pulling the paper aside when I woke up. I lay in bed for a minute and blinked the dream away. It was a good Dragon's Mass Eve. But it was twenty five years behind me now and the truth I swallowed made my stomach hurt.

I looked up to the picture of my mother

that had hung above my bed since the night he'd first given it to me.

I forced myself up and drew a bath. When I walked past my father's open door, I did not let myself look in upon his empty bed, upon the spectacles that lay on his nightstand, folded closed and never to be opened again by his large, clumsy fingers.

> *Muscles tire. It's all we really knew. The dragon's back held up the world. The poetry and faith of the Singing Literocrats held up the dragon by the will of the Sixteen Princes. One Literocrat fell to the sword, another to plague, a third to famine. Halved in this way, the choir faltered in its song and the dragon caved in on its spindly legs. The Sixteen Princes had no time to act, to change the course of this sudden, sweeping end. They drank wine and spoke of lemon trees instead.*
>
> *We sat in the cold until the Santaman came.*
>
> —*The Breaking of the Dragon's Back*
>   *The Santaman Cycle,*
>   Authorized Standard Version
>   Verity Press, 2453 YD

THE FIRST WEEK CREPT BY WITH varied weather. Storms of sorrow blew in at the slightest provocation—the smell of him on his clothes, his pen laid carefully to the left side of his desk blotter, the notes he'd written and organized for me. And on the heels of the sadness, a calm and foreboding hollowness that I didn't know I could feel. Followed suddenly by inconsolable rage that had no place to go but inward or else it might burn down the world.

I went through the pile of papers, mailing what needed mailed and making the calls on Father's list. I loaded the granite marker he'd kept in the mine all these years onto the wagon and drove it into town. He'd had his name and birthdate carved onto it when he had mother's made. *The rest is up to you*, his note told me. And so I dropped it with Anderson, Bauer and Sons' Stonework, picked it up a week later, and planted it at the head of the fresh grave.

Drummond Angus Farrelly, it said, along with his dates of birth and death. *Public servant, cherished father, beloved husband.*

The government men showed up about a month after, briefcases in hands.

"Miss Farrelly?" the man in the suit asked when I opened the door.

"Ms. Sheffleton-Farrelly," I corrected

him. "Melody. Call me Mel."

The man looked uncomfortable and his partner looked away, clearing his voice. Their pinstriped trousers and jackets looked out of place here on the edge of the world and I wasn't sure how they kept their shoes so shiny. "Is there someplace we can talk?"

I nodded toward my father's office—a shack near the gated entrance of the mine. I dried my hands and laid my dish towel over a wooden chair. "Across the way," I said.

I led us across the hard-packed yard and used the key to open the door. There had been little to do in the office and I'd spent most of my time here arranging and re-arranging the items on his desk.

I sat behind it now, still feeling dwarfed by its size, and waited until my guests sat. They each placed their cases across their knees and opened them. "First," the spokesman said as he lifted out an accordion file of papers, "let me say how sorry we all were to hear about Drum's—your father's—passing. I worked with him on several procurements and had a lot of respect for him."

"Thank you." My father, in addition to his contract for the mine, had also entered into consulting contracts with the Bureaucracy from time to time, leaving me with either the Gustavsons or the Graves—sometimes for months at a time—to ride east and do his part to help put the world right. I'd always hoped to go with him, but for one reason or another, we never made it happen. But I'd write my stories as if I'd gone, weaving tales of our derring-do and heroics on secret missions for the Bureaucracy.

"That said," the government man continued, "there are uncomfortable matters to discuss."

I nodded. I knew of at least one matter—the pension. Father thought he'd found a loophole that would allow it to pass to me—something about a Board Order from the past century regarding widows and orphans. But I'd read the order and didn't think it was likely to work in my case. "The pension, right?"

He nodded. "Yes. I'm afraid you do not meet the age requirements for survivorship to apply."

"Understood," I said.

"And then there is the matter of the mining contract."

My eyes came up to his. "The mining contract?"

His smile was apologetic as he drew a letter out of the file. "Unfortunately, amendment six removed the assignment clause from the Bureaucracy's standard terms and conditions. Which means that with the passing of your father—the contractor in this regard—this contract is null and void. I've a letter of cancellation for you, notarized by the Board clerk."

I felt anger rising in my face. "Amendment six?" I rolled my chair to the file cabinet to my left and pulled open the second drawer. "When was this amendment issued? I don't recall seeing it. Do you have an executed copy?"

He shook his head. "It's just been issued in the last fortnight. But unfortunately, Mr. Farrelly is no longer in a position to . . ." Here he cleared his voice and looked away. "To sign it."

Red tape. My father had created his share of it in the Bureaucracy's basement.

I smiled. "Surely you can re-compete it." The first ten years, father had operated the mine on a no-bid contract. It was the only operating hope mine in the western provinces and that made it eligible for a sole source exemption. But the last two and a half decades, he'd competed for it. No one else had, so of course he was awarded the contract.

Red tape.

The government man shook his head. "We are not going to re-procure in this case, Ms. Sheffleton-Farrelly. As you know, the Drawler threat in the north is taking more and more resources. The Bureaucracy is cutting expenses wherever it can."

I leaned forward. "Are you giving up on hope altogether then?"

"No," he said. "We'll fund mining efforts elsewhere certainly where it makes sense."

"Just not here."

"Not here," he agreed. Then, he leaned forward. "Ms. Sheffleton-Farrelly, do you have any idea when the last time was that this mine produced a single flake of hope?"

I rolled back to the file cabinet, this time opening the top drawer to pull out the production journals. "Late autumn," I said. "Twenty-six-fifty-three, Year of the Dragon."

It was the same year my father had gone to seminary.

"Eighty years," the man said. "And thirty-five of them subsidized by tax dollars with nothing to show for it."

There was little to say after that. They left me with a stack of papers less than an hour later, climbing into their jeep and driving back to the town's single inn.

I went over those papers that afternoon, filing them carefully like he would have, and afterward, I adjusted father's

If Dragon's Mass Eve Be Cold and Clear 37

financial projections less his ongoing pension payments and the contract revenue. I checked his notations in the savings ledger one last time before folding it up and tucking it back into the file cabinet. If I were frugal, I had maybe two years left here. And after that?

There was a form in the paperwork from the Bureaucracy—an application for the civil service exam with a box already marked and initialed on it, authorizing me to take the test in any satellite branch where it was offered and extending bonus points based on my relationship to one Drummond Angus Farrelly, a decorated procurement officer.

I filed it separate from the other papers and snuffed out the lamp. I looked over everything, neatly in its place, before locking the office door. After today, I really wasn't sure when I'd be back.

Then I went up to father's grave for the first time since digging it. I sat heavily upon the ground and leaned against his marker. "You were wrong about the pension," I told him. "The mining contract, too."

And in that moment, I was certain I heard his voice. First, he chuckled. Then, he told me what he'd told me so many times before.

"Being right," my father reminded me, "is not always required."

Myth became life. No one really believed in the Santaman until he came with his tattered red robe and his dripping red sword. No one really believed in his undying love until he burst into our direst need to carve us a new home from the bones of the world.

We looked up at the whistle of his wolf-stallion. "Why do you weep and whimper?" the Santaman asked from the back of his mount.

"We whimper for the end of our world," one of us said. "We weep for the fall of the Singing Literocrats and the Breaking of the Dragon's Back."

The Santaman grinned and shook his sword. Blood rained down from it, mixing with the ashes. "Weep also for the Sixteen Princes who have failed you."

"Why, Lord?" someone asked.

The Santaman spun his mount. "For I have avenged you in the Name Above All and they are no more."

We did not waver in our weeping. There was no lull in our lament.

—*The Coming of the Santaman*
   The Santaman Cycle,
   Authorized Standard Version
   Verity Press, 2453 YD

In grief, time moves at inconsistent pace and the bereaved adjust and shuffle forward accordingly. I did not return to my father's grave again for nearly two years, though I watched it often from the kitchen window or from the yard.

Each month, I hitched the wagon and went into town to re-supply. And on each trip, I endured the sympathy of the closest thing we had to a community so far removed from the rest of the world.

"What will you do now?" was the most popular question, and I never had a real answer. I took their offered condolences and tucked them away. And I watched the numbers on the savings ledger shrink.

I pulled the pictures from the Cycle and tucked the book away out of sight, moving the photographs into the treasure box I kept beneath my bed. But after that, I left the box where it lay for a long time and let it find its dust.

I wouldn't have known the season but for news of the fighting in the north. More

Black Drawlers leaking into the world through the ether, moving further south in their hunger. And when I knew the day approached, I even went into town to collect what jars and cans I could.

The mercantile even had red paper, and I bought a sheet.

But as Dragon's Mass Eve drew near, the knot in my stomach grew tighter and my eyes went more often to the hill. Finally, I surrendered and found the best dress that still fit me and rode into town.

Father had never taken me to the church for Dragon's Mass Eve, but we'd visited one Dragonsday for weekly services. On the ride in, I sat beside him on the bench and we talked about what we were going to see.

"There won't be many, I'll wager," he said. "But there will be some. Parson Brown will pray and Emily Hopewell will play a few hymns on the organ that we will all sing to. Then, the parson will preach about the Santaman and take a collection."

When we arrived, the parson's eyes lit

up. "Drum Farrelly," he said, "you're just about the last person I expected to show up this morning."

I remember my father's strained smile as he shook the parson's hand. "Melody was curious," he said.

I'd seen Parson Brown around town, but never in the dark robes of his priesthood. It made the short, round man look almost comical. He'd shaken my hand, looking up at me with a smile. "Welcome," he said.

We took our seat on the back row.

Then, just as father said, we prayed and sang and listened and sang again and as we did, father slipped a small wad of the most recently authorized currency into the plate that passed up and down the pews of scattered faithful.

On the ride home, we'd had our discussion and father dissected the components of the service.

"At the end," I told him, "they prayed for the Santaman's return. Do they do it every Dragonsday?"

He nodded. "Some of them do it *every* day."

"Not just on Dragon's Mass Eve?"

"No."

"But they believe one day it will work?"

"Yes."

"They really *really* believe?"

He nodded again. "They really *really* believe. And I used to, too. Even your mother, in some ways, believed. Only she believed that if there was a Santaman, he expected us to work while we waited and make things as good as we could." He looked thoughtful for a moment.

"But we don't believe now," I said.

He smiled at me. "*I* don't believe now. Do you?"

I smiled back. "No, I really don't. I think. . ." I tried to find something to hitch my thought to. I remembered the growing stack of bound cardboard covers he kept in the drawer beside his bed, each containing my carefully written pages of our fictional misadventures spread out over a half-dozen Dragon's Mass Eves. "I think it's a good story, but I don't think it's true." Then, I said what I knew he was going to say next. "But I suppose being true isn't always required."

He smiled. "Exactly so."

I blinked tears away at the memory as I turned the corner onto Main Street and saw the brightly lit building that waited.

Parson Brown stood at the door and smiled at me. "Mel Farrelly," he said. "You're just about the last person I expected to show up tonight."

I climbed down and hitched my horse. "Happy Dragon's Mass Eve, Parson," I said as I took his hand.

"And to you," he said.

The church was full, with men and women crowded onto the pews in their Dragonsday best. I spotted the Gustavsons and the Graves near the middle of the overflowing sanctuary, and though both families waved me over, I took a spot in the last row in the back corner. My nervous hands picked up the worn hymnal and thumbed through the pages until the parson took to the pulpit and offered the invocation.

After, there was a small choir that sang a medley of hymns. The room joined in and it was nothing like the scattered voices I'd heard in this very room as a child—it was one voice made of many, booming out into the night in a cry for help that I could nearly give myself over to. But I did not want help from some mysterious, red-cloaked and red-bladed avenger. I wanted my father, and the power of that longing flooded my eyes with tears. Still, when we reached "If Dragon's Mass Eve Be Cold and Clear," I sang the original words—the writer's words—and not the softer *maybe* his hymn had been neutered into.

"Now tonight," Parson Brown intoned after the singing, "we have a special treat."

My first thought was that he meant to introduce me, point me out to the crowd, and I found myself suddenly wanting to flee. But it didn't happen. Instead, he nodded to a young man who sat to the side. "Tonight," Parson Brown said, "Brother

Simon will bring the homily. His first sermon, I might add."

A wave of murmurs rolled over the congregation, and I pressed my mouth together, studying the young man.

His robes were ill-fitting and his eyebrows and cheekbones bore a hint of the fey. He took the pulpit, thumbing through the leather-bound copy of the Cycle that he carried to it, and he smiled out at us. "Good evening," he said as Parson Brown took a seat behind him. "Tonight's message is taken from the Coming of the Santaman, verses one through three."

As he read the scripture, I mouthed the words with him. "Myth became life," he read. "No one really believed in the Santaman until he came with his tattered red robe and his dripping red sword. No one really believed in his undying love until he burst into our direst need to carve us a new home from the bones of the world."

Brother Simon closed the book and looked upon us all. When his eyes moved over the back pew, they met mine and I felt the measurement in his level gaze. "I submit to you, brothers and sisters, that like those before us, we do not *really* believe in the Santaman."

From there, he launched into his sermon and I found his words fading and blurring, taking a seat behind him like the parson, as he filled the room with his presence. His hands moved like a magician, illustrating this or that point, indicating this or that observation, as he moved across the platform. His voice was hypnotic, rising and falling in passion and pitch, and his eyes continued wandering the crowded room, finding mine on more than one occasion. Those eyes, I knew, were unsafe. They held too many contradicting views—hope and fear, anger and grace, and something more I'd never been comfortable with: Conviction.

When he finished, he sat down abruptly and Parson Brown took over. After singing "The Santman Shall Rise Again" as the plate migrated up and down the rows, he dismissed us to the fellowship hall for cookies and tea.

I was moving toward the door when Brother Simon caught up to me and shook my hand. The hand was rough and calloused; it caught me off guard. "You're not leaving are you?"

I blushed and stammered but didn't know why. "I have . . . things to do."

"Come have a cookie at least." Then, as an afterthought: "I'm Simon by the way." And somehow, the voice compelled me, and I let him guide me by the elbow into the fellowship hall before he vanished into the crowd.

A cup of tea was pushed into one of my hands, a molasses cookie into the other, and I blessed both because it meant I need not shake any more hands.

I stood quietly in the corner and suffered the kindness and curiosity of a town that had seen little of me and little of my father before me.

I'd finished the tea and moved for the door when the parson came by with the young man in tow. "And this," he said, "is

Melody Farrelly. She owns the old hope mine out past the Gustavson's farm."

"We've met," I said and forced a smile. But I shook his offered hand again, noticing once more how rough it was.

"Brother Simon is our new acolyte. He's in his last year at the Middleton Seminary. I expect he'll be taking my place when I retire next year." He turned to the young man. "Melody's father, Drummond, spent a year at Middleton."

His face lit up. "Is he here with you?"

I looked away. "He passed away last Dragon's Mass Eve."

The light dimmed and his smile faded. "I'm sorry."

"I've been meaning to ask," the Parson said. "Do you know what you will do now? Will you sell the mine?"

I shrugged. "It hasn't produced in over eighty years. Not much demand for a hope mine without hope."

And then, the conversation folded in on itself and the two of them moved on. I excused myself and slipped out under a cloudy night to find my horse.

I rode home and tried to eat at least some of the fruit salad I'd made earlier that day. It tasted empty without my father. And I knew better than to recite the Cycle. Instead, I braved his room—something I rarely brought myself to do—and curled up on his large bed. Then, I pulled open the drawer and pulled out the stack of stories I'd written him through the years.

As I read them, I found myself laughing and crying, and when I felt sleep pulling at me, I gathered them up and took them to my own room. I pulled out the cardboard box beneath my bed and laid them carefully in it.

My eyes caught the wadded up piece of paper I'd also tucked into the box, and I forced them away. That ball of paper was the first to go into my treasure box, though I couldn't bring myself to open it up and smooth it out. It made me too angry and too afraid.

But now, a strange fancy struck me, and I lifted it careful as a butterfly from a flower. I sat on my bed and held it, remembering my last conversation with my father. Then, I smoothed it out upon my lap.

It was a requisition slip, filled out and in triplicate. He'd completed most of it, leaving the order date blank along with the boxes used to select gender.

Then, I remembered the words I'd said to him—off and on for years—and the quiet way he smiled when I said them.

"I don't want a child," I told the empty room.

Then, I placed the smoothed-out form in the box and lowered the lid over it like a casket before laying it to rest again in the dusty grave beneath my bed.

Dust rose from the West as the Santaman approached. The wolf-stallion growled and tore sod and the last of the Literocrats lay down their lyres by the Murmuring Stream as the dragon's eye faltered above them.

"Take up your tools and lift your song," the Santaman cried.

"We are halved," the Fourth Literocrat said. "Our song is lost. The world ends. The dragon's back, already broken."

The sword licked out, then pointed North. The Murmuring Stream ran pink. "Sing a new home," the Santaman cried again. "Beyond the ether at the Edge of the World."

Two voices rose and fell in song. A third burbled in the stream. Scooping the golden-haired head from the water, the Santaman came seeking us to tell us of our new carved home.

> —*The Last of the Literocrats*
> *The Santaman Cycle,*
> Authorized Standard Version
> Verity Press, 2453 YD

The next year moved faster. I learned that loss is like a hole in the middle of your living room floor. Your rearrange the furniture around it and you visit it once in awhile but less and less often with every month. Eventually, you grow accustomed to walking around the hole, living around it as it just becomes a part of your life.

I started writing again, though I'd long ago outgrown the adventure stories I used to tell. Instead, I wrote about my father and about my memories of him. I tended the garden and stretched the savings as far as I could. And in the weeks before Dragon's Mass Eve, as the news turned somber in the north, I didn't even try to find the canned fruits and vegetables and meat. But I did slip into his office to fill out the civil service exam application. I put it into an envelope and took it into the house.

I still wasn't certain if I would mail it.

When Dragon's Mass Eve arrived, I rode into town again and like the year before, I slipped onto the back pew. The church was less crowded this year and when Parson Brown's invocation included a blessing upon the men and women serving in the local militia, I made the connection with why.

The singing was more subdued, and when Brother Simon took the pulpit, there was something quiet about him that felt disconnected from the young man I'd seen prowling the platform a year before. "Tonight's message," he said, "is taken from the Last of the Literocrats, verses one through five."

We made eye contact as he read, and the light I'd seen before was dark now. There was something of sorrow or anger in them now that resonated with me, and I couldn't look away.

"Take up your tools and lift your song," he said. "That is what I want to talk about with you tonight."

What followed were brief but heartfelt comments, but nothing like the lively performance I knew he was capable of. When we shook hands later, in the fellowship hall,

I could even feel the difference in his grip. And the hands were less rough here in the second year of his apprenticeship.

"I enjoyed your message," I told him, even more uncomfortable with his eyes in such close proximity. "My mother used to believe that the Santaman wouldn't return until we'd done our very best with our own hands."

He nodded and smiled, but I saw the falseness in it. "Yes," he said. There were clouds behind those eyes now, too.

I leaned close to him and lowered my voice. "Are you okay, Brother Simon?"

He looked at me, and I think he was surprised that I noticed, though it was as obvious as his nose to me. His cheeks grew red and he looked around, panic on his face.

Finally, he pulled me aside, and his words were fast and jumbled together. "We lost Fallowston and Reinburg this morning," he said. "The diocese sent a rider. The crier will be announcing it tomorrow. Parson Brown didn't want to dampen spirits tonight with the news."

I knew the towns though I'd never visited them. "Did you have people there?"

He shook his head. "No. But our militia is engaged at Candletoss." I imagined the points on the map, saw how close it all was.

Simon looked out the window and I saw the firmness in his jawline and the anger in his eyes. Outside, it was a clear night and I understood his anger better.

"Something," he said, "has to happen soon."

I nodded but didn't know what to say. Finally, I found my voice. "Maybe," I said, "it's like you said earlier—maybe we're called upon to take up our tools and lift our song. Especially when we're faced with the end of our world . . . just like the Last of the Literocrats."

"Yes. Maybe."

Then he was moving off into the crowd, shaking hands and patting shoulders. I slipped out beneath a star-scattered sky and rode home in the light of the moons.

When I reached the homestead, I stabled my horse and slipped into the house. I found the envelope first, and then I went to the box beneath my bed and pulled out the wadded-up requisition slip. Taking both, I let myself back out into the night and climbed the hill behind the house.

I sat quietly for a while, prayerless and facing north. "I don't know if it's the right thing to do," I told my father, "but I'm going to do it. I know you were right about most things—all the important things, really—and I think you were right about this. But I'm still afraid."

I paused in that moment and knew I would have given everything I owned to have this one final conversation with him, to hear his words and see his eyes as he formed them. But in thirty-five years with the old troll, I knew what he would ask next and I blushed.

"No," I said. "I don't know *who* yet." Still, I knew who I'd thought about the few times I'd let myself imagine it. "Regardless of who, I'm going to do it and I wanted you to know. But I'm going to have to leave you to make it happen. Because I'm also going to take the test."

I reached out then to touch the gravestone. The granite felt wrong to my fingertips and I rubbed them into the stone, feeling something powdery flaking off as I did.

My first thought was that it was ash or dust. But my second thought was the one that brought my fingers tentatively to my mouth. I'd never tasted hope before, but my father had described it many times before.

Bitter and sweet at the same time.

I looked above me at the clear night and stood on shaking legs. I went into the house and lit the lantern, grabbed my knife, and lifted the keys to the mine off the hook where my father had last hung them.

I walked down into the mine, and I hadn't gone very far when the dark walls started to glisten white. I paused along the way to scrape here or there, each time coming away with a handful of white flaky residue.

I went all the way to the bottom, and when I reached it, I sat down and laughed until my sides hurt, and then I cried until my eyes had no more tears in them.

Two days later, I phoned in my requisition at the town's single phone, dialing the number my father gave me. And when I finished with central stores, I had the operator transfer me to the contracts division.

"North of the faraway beyond the ether at the Edge of the World" the head sang and died. The Santaman cast it aside.

"The way is too hard," we told the Santaman. *"And we are afraid."*

He sheathed his sword and climbed down among us. He cast open his arms, his red robes hung like bleeding meat. "Do not be afraid. I walk with you."

North, he walked his wolf-stallion, and we followed after. In twilight, we walked, and as the ruined cities fell behind us, others joined our ragged band.

Lost also behind us, the last of the literocrats sang sunrise and sunset, sang muscles and sinew, sang bones and teeth.

Death crabs scuttled and scavenged. Snick-snack went the sword.

Black Drawlers shrieked and savaged. Snick-snack went the sword.

Some of us fell. Some of us faltered. All of us hoped.

The faraway wrapped us and the ash snows fell away.

Sunlight bathed us and we swam out into the ether at the Edge of the World.

Swam towards our new carved home.

—*The Ether at the Edge of the World*
   The Santaman Cycle,
   Authorized Standard Version
   Verity Press, 2453 YD

If Dragon's Mass Eve Be Cold and Clear

THE BUREAUCRACY WAS FASTER THIS time. Within two weeks, the suits were back. They offered twenty years, but I declined, much to their surprise. "One year is about as far ahead as I can see for now," I said.

They looked nervous when I said that. "Do you have other plans for the mine?"

I shrugged. "I might sell it. And I would certainly want to entertain a bid from the Bureaucracy if it comes to that."

My reassurance helped, and when they left, I went to my father's savings ledger and readjusted the figures to account for the contract income. Tomorrow, I'd ride into town and hire a small crew.

A knock at the office door brought my head up. Brother Simon stood framed in the late morning light. "Miss Farrelly," he said with a nod.

"Ms. Sheffleton-Farrelly," I corrected him. "Call me Mel."

"Mel," he said. "May I come in?"

I nodded. ""Please," I said, pointing

to a chair. "Sit. I didn't know parsons still made house calls."

He blushed. "I'm not a parson."

"You will be soon enough."

Simon shook his head. "No, I've stepped down. I don't think I'm made for the priesthood."

I'd seen him just two weeks before, and even in that short time, whatever crisis he'd been working through seemed more settled and calm. I knew it was none of my business, and it was a question that I hated, but I asked it anyway. "Then what will do you now?"

He looked around the room and then our eyes met. "What I used to do. I was apprenticed to a blacksmith before."

I nodded and looked at his hands. "So you're traveling the parish and letting everyone know?"

He shook his head. "No. Just you for now."

My breath caught, and for a moment, I wondered if he somehow knew about some of the thoughts I'd thought about him on cold nights beneath my quilt. But I quickly kicked my imagination back to quiet; it was an awkward quiet.

Simon filled it. "I heard you struck hope."

I laughed. "I didn't strike it; it struck me. My father seeded this place for three seasons and got nothing. Then, decades later . . ." I snapped my fingers in the air. "Hope."

"Hope," he said. "I need some actually."

I studied him. "I have some. How much do you need?"

"A pound," he said. "I . . . I don't have any money."

A pound was a lot. Not for me at the moment, but a pound of hope in a world that had for too long gone without . . . its value was staggering. "What are you going to do with it?"

"I'm borrowing Jansen's shop at night," he said. His face went red again and he looked around the empty room as if to make sure no one could hear him. "I'm re-forging the Santaman's sword."

I sat back, surprised. "You're what?"

He nodded. "I'm re-forging the sword based on its description in the Doctrines and Affirmations. I'm going to take it north."

I raised my eyebrows. "Why would you do that?"

"Because maybe if he sees we've tried ... really tried ... maybe then he'll hear."

I shook my head. "Simon," I said, "I don't think the Santaman's listening."

But when our eyes met this time, I knew it didn't matter. His conviction was back, and now it bent him away from words and motions, moved him toward deeds and demonstrations now, but it was still the same drive for miracles and wonders to flow into and out of his life. "Please," he said. "I can't do it without hope."

I sighed and measured him. "Okay. But I want something for it."

"Anything I have that I can give you," he said.

I smiled. "Come back tonight for dinner, Simon, and we'll talk about it. I'll have the hope ready for you."

After he left, I weighed out two pounds from the hope I'd scraped these past two weeks. I filled a small sack with it and locked up. Then, I went inside to get ready.

I put a chicken on to roast and took a long bath. I brushed out my hair, and when none of my dresses fit right, I put on trousers and a cotton button-up shirt. I smiled at myself in the tiny mirror, grateful that I couldn't see my entire body in its reflection. I'd gotten many of my mother's features, but I had my father's broad shoulders and thickness along with his towering height.

When Simon knocked at the door, the house smelled of chicken and fresh baked bread. Clouds had wandered in and blotted out the starlight, but the temperature was still down and he was shivering. I let him in and took his coat. "Did you walk?"

He nodded. "I don't have a horse."

I hefted the bag of hope. "I'll just put this with your coat."

"Thank you."

Nothing I did felt right, and my father's words—right was not required—brought little comfort. I wasn't sure what to say or what to do, and it was obvious to me that I was the only one who comprehended the potential of this night. I set the table while we made small talk, and then I opened the bottle of bumbleberry wine I'd kept for such a night as this. I poured out small glassfuls and dished up our plates.

We ate quickly and I watched him. He talked throughout, and I finished easily ahead of him because of it. I think somewhere in the midst of it he must've noticed how I looked at him and it made him talk all the more, his nervous words bumping into each other in their rush to get out.

Finally, I took his plate to the sink along with my own. We moved to the battered old sofa in the living room and sat before the fire. I refilled our wine glasses.

"So you wanted to talk about price," he said.

I sipped the wine, set it down and nodded. "I do. And it's okay to say no. You can have the hope either way."

His brow furrowed. "Say no to what?"

I held my breath and leaned my face toward him. "This."

Then, I kissed him.

At first, he did nothing. Then, he kissed me back. And after a moment, he broke away. "I'm sorry," he said. "I don't know . . . I can't—"

I withdrew and felt the sting of the panic on his face. "No," I said. "I'm sorry." I stood, feeling small for the first time in my life. "Like I said—it's okay to say no."

He stood, too, his face and ears bright red. "No, that's not what I mean." He swallowed, stepped closer to me and stretched up on tippy-toes to kiss my mouth. "It's just that I've never done this before."

Relief flooded me. "Oh," I said. Now it was my turn to blush. "I haven't either."

"Really?"

I nodded. "Really." Then, I bent down and kissed him back.

Taking his hand, I led him to my fresh-made bed and we spent the night teaching each other how.

I never told him why. I couldn't see how it would help him at all, and I could count a dozen ways that it might hurt him. Instead, I just enjoyed him and helped him to enjoy me.

In the morning, after breakfast, he walked back into town with a smile on his face and a bag of hope slung over his shoulder.

And in the north, he'll hear our cry
Ride forth in wrath, his sword raised high
To carve our home in violent grace
And lead us to that promised place

   —*Hymn #316,*
     "The Santaman Shall Rise Again"
     Hymns of the Dragon and his Avenger,
     Contemporary Edition
     Verity Music, 2623 YD

It was only after that night with Simon that I allowed myself to think about my last conversation with Father. I'm not sure why, but I don't need the why's nearly as much as I used to when I was younger.

It was morning when he called me to his room. He'd soiled himself again and after nearly a month in bed, I was just beginning to realize that I might not have even another year with him.

I pretended I wasn't angry and tried to find my patience, but it waned. He knew me well enough to know I was frustrated and I suspected he even knew why—it wasn't the mess in his bed. It was the mess my life would become when he left it and I couldn't bear to face that.

I spent the morning cleaning him up and then cleaning his sheets. When I went into the kitchen and saw the cans and jars laid out, preparing for Dragon's Mass Eve was the last thing I wanted to be doing.

"Come in here, Mel," my father rumbled from his bedroom.

I sighed and felt my pulse rising. "What do you need, Dad?"

His laugh was more of a bark. "I need *you.*"

I wanted to snap at him but I didn't. Instead, I closed my eyes, counted to five, and then went to his doorway. "Yes?"

He sat up in bed, his lap covered with open books—not real books but bits of cardboard bound together with yarn. "You should write more of these someday," he said. "They're good."

I shrugged. "Is that what you needed?"

He shook his head. "No. Come here." He patted the bed beside him.

If Dragon's Mass Eve Be Cold and Clear 71

I went to the side of the bed but didn't sit. "I have a meal to cook," I said.

Our eyes met. "Sit," he said. "I'm not hungry."

"It's Dragon's Mass Eve and—"

"Sit down, Mel." He looked old there, but truth be told, I couldn't remember a time when my father didn't. He was in his sixties when I was born.

I sat and felt the bed creak beneath our combined weight. "What?"

He smiled. "I wanted to give you your Dragon's Mass Eve present."

"Let's wait until tonight," I said. "I don't have yours ready yet."

Father shook his head and a fit of coughing took his words for a minute. "I don't want to wait," he said. "As tired as I've been, I'm likely to sleep through Dragon's Mass Eve anyway."

I forced a smile. "Okay. But you get yours tomorrow if you fall asleep."

He shrugged, then leaned over to dig around within the deep drawer in the nightstand. He pulled out a form—in triplicate—and handed it to me. "This," he said, "is for you."

I looked at it. I rubbed my eyes and looked at it again. "What's this?"

He cleared his voice. "It's ... urm ... a requisition slip. I've been saving it for you. Your mother and I brought two with us when we rode west."

I read it, my eyes naturally drawn to the places where he'd taken the liberty of filling it out. As I realized what it was, I felt the anger burning hot in me and by instinct, I crumpled the requisition into as tight a ball as my white knuckled fist could make it. "I don't want a child," I said. "I don't *ever* want a child."

I tried to stand, but his gnarled hand caught my arm and I turned on him. I nearly said something, nearly let the feelings that savaged me slip past my careful control. But I kept quiet. Still, he saw everything in my eyes, and his own filled up with tears at the sight of my anger.

"I'm sorry," he said.

"Why?" I asked.

He blinked. "Why am I sorry?"

I shook my head. "No," I said. "Why do you think I should have a child?" Seeing his tears made my own fight harder to get out.

He patted my arm. "I thought when I met your mother that I knew what love was. But meeting *you* opened up a vast continent of love I never imagined could exist. How could I not want that for you?" His voice lowered, and then my father said the last words that he would ever say to me. "Melody Constance Sheffleton-Farrelly, don't you know that you are the best gift anyone ever gave to me, Dragon's Mass Eve or not?"

I stood and bent to kiss his brow. Then, I left so he wouldn't see me crying. I tossed the ball of paper into my room and went outside into the yard to walk off the feelings that ambushed me. When I went back inside, I saw my father had gone to sleep amid the stories I'd written him over a lifetime of Dragon's Mass Eves together. And when I checked on him even later, I found he'd slipped away.

I gathered up the books, closed them, and stacked them neatly in his nightstand drawer. I carefully removed his spectacles and folded them up to lay them beside his bed.

Then I went to find something to wrap him in and wondered if the coming night would be cloudy or clear.

Motes swim. Light diffuses. Home rises.

We see it through a smoky glass. We watch it twitch and meep with each note of the framing song.

The Santaman laughs and beats his sword against his thigh: "Ho, ho, ho."

We few remaining weep and set our feet on emerald grass. We smell the reek of love upon the wind. We wipe our eyes. We wipe our eyes and look again.

Ahead a dragon.

Upon his back a world.

—*Our New Carved Home*
  The Santaman Cycle,
  Authorized Standard Version
  Verity Press, 2453 YD

YOU ARRIVED IN AUTUMN AMID THE buzz of change.

But before that, while I waited for you, I started wrapping things up at our homestead on the edge of the world. I went through my father's papers and organized them, separating out his working notes from his personal notes. Most, I kept. But some I left for the mine's new owners.

I felt you kick for the first time while I was taking the civil service exam, and after I finished, the test proctor sought me out in the waiting room after everyone else had gone to let me know he'd not seen a score so high in well over twenty years.

I wasn't surprised at all when the offer came through, and once it did, I started negotiating the sale of the mine. I knew going in that whatever I sold it for would be vastly more than I could make in a lifetime on government salary, working in the cubicle maze of the Bureaucracy. But a clean start seemed somehow right to me, especially as your arrival drew closer and closer.

Still, I'm glad we had these three months together on the homestead where we both were born. Wandering the yard, it's been a strange, new mourning as I accept the reality that I'll likely not come back here again. You may when you're older. You might want to see where your

If Dragon's Mass Eve Be Cold and Clear 77

grandmother and grandfather lay buried. You may want to see the house where you were born. And I'm sure folks around here will be curious to meet you, too.

There is a knock at the door on the morning of Dragon's Mass Eve and it startles you. I go to answer and find Parson Brown on the porch. He sees the truck the Bureaucracy has provided me, shoved full of everything we'll take with us when we leave. I've only left out enough to celebrate tonight, and tomorrow, we start our weeks-long drive east and south.

"So," he says, "you really are going?"

I nod. "Tomorrow," I say. "Come in, Parson."

I brew him some tea while he plays with you and I can tell you're as uncomfortable with him as he is with you. When the tea is ready, I hold you while he drinks it, mindful of his shaking hands. I want to ask him about your father, but I don't. Last I heard, he'd ridden north with his sword and not long after, bits of gossip drifted back. I don't know who exactly wields it, but there are rumors of a young man in red with a terrible blade, and he's earning quite a name for himself. I'm pretty sure it's him. But maybe it isn't. Maybe someone further north heard the cry of his heart. I doubt it, but it would be a fine story.

Drawler season didn't really subside this year—they pushed south all the way through summer—but the militias are holding them at Harrowfield and Lumner, and in a few weeks, I'll be working supply chain for the headquarters of a new standing army.

I don't ask about your father. And I don't tell Parson Brown your middle name is Simon, either. I know people are wondering and I'm okay with letting them wonder.

I look into your eyes and I find I could fall into them. They are brown like mine and like your grandfather's. The parson has to ask a second time before I realize he's speaking. "I'm sorry?"

"I was asking if you'd be joining us tonight," he says as he drains the last of his tea.

If Dragon's Mass Eve Be Cold and Clear 79

"I've a new acolyte. Brother Timothy. He'll be giving the sermon." Parson Brown leans forward and tickles your chin. "I'm sure everyone is dying to meet little Drummond."

I smile. "Maybe," I tell him. "We'll see."

But I already know we won't be attending. Tonight, I'll make our hats, and after I've nursed you, I'll eat rice stew and fruit salad. Then, we'll walk up the hill and I will hold you close as I recite words that don't need to be right or true to have their meaning for me. For us.

I think I understand my father's last Dragon's Mass Eve gift to me now when I see his face in yours. His attachment to his old, discarded religion makes sense to me now, too, though I had to meet you before I could fully comprehend the truest object of his faith.

Clear or cloudy, the only grace I'll ever need has already found me.

And the only home I'll ever want is you.

THE DOOM OF LOVE IN SMALL SPACES

W E MET AT WORK.
She looked at me when she walked into the room and I was immediately untethered. Pretty brunette in a red dress who *knew* she was pretty, knew that the thigh-high slit along the side of her skirt and the haphazard plummet of her neckline were reefs where men could be shipwrecked. Her flashing eyes sang danger and peace in two-part harmony. Each step towards me delivered the unrelenting clip-clap, clip-clap of heels across a tile floor so brightly polished that it reflected back her matching red panties.

I held my breath and waited to catch fire from the sight of her.

"Central Supply," she said when she stood in front of my desk. Her voice melted the crystalline sugar on my glazed donut. I watched it puddle and pool on the paper napkin.

I swallowed. "That's me, Miss."

She smiled. "Just you?"

I nodded. Now my styrofoam cup started bending from the heat of her, tilting precariously. The coffee inside it bubbled. "Just me."

She leaned over my desk and bent slightly, tipping her breasts toward me. They hung, held in place by a red bra. "I need more love," she said. "We've run completely out on the fifth floor."

The hair on my arms curled in on itself, the stink of burning in my nose alongside her floral perfume and her peppermint breath. I forced my eyes to her face, squinting to see her through the haze of smoke.

"Are you okay?" she asked.

My tongue expanded in my mouth, swelling to block my words. I forced it back to normal size. "You must be new?"

She threw back her shoulders and tossed her hair. "Not so much." Her teeth shined now, fine and white and straight. "We just don't use a lot of supplies anymore on the fifth floor. I think the last person

The Doom of Love in Small Spaces

they sent down was Bill when they ran out of hope."

I remembered Bill. He'd dragged himself in here and died in the corner before he could tell me what he wanted. It wasn't the first time. Wouldn't be the last. "I remember Bill," I said. "Good chap."

"Dead chap," she said.

I shrugged and motioned to the chair beside my desk. "It happens a lot around here."

She sat and crossed her legs. The slit fell open like a theater curtain. Long, slender legs, white heat shimmering off them to singe my eyebrows.

"So you need some love," I said, opening my card file and thumbing through the microfiche.

She folded her hands in her lap. "Please."

"How much?"

"Well, as much as you can spare."

I slipped the flimsy plastic film into the reader and hit the switch. A blue field swimming with white letters blurred into focus with the turn of a knob.

I watched her out of the corner of my eye. She pulled self-consciously at her bra-strap and fidgeted. "Elevators still out?" I asked, trying to make small talk.

She nodded. "Board says they're not repairing them, either."

"Bloody barkers," I said. Of course, she had no way of knowing that I was the one who told them not to repair the elevators. Working elevators meant the rapid movement of supplies up and down the building. I'd sent the memo in, followed all the usual forms. Naturally, they'd listened to me.

They had to.

I moved the arm of the microfiche reader, sliding the film over the light. "Love," I said. "Any particular size or shape?"

"Love comes in shapes and sizes?" she asked.

"All," I said.

She answered me with a laugh.

"We're out," I lied. I had a smallish off-brand muzzled and leashed in the back of the storeroom that I'd left off the inventory. "But we could order some."

She stood, came around my desk so she could read over my shoulder. She leaned in to me and I felt her breath on my neck. "How long?"

I shrugged. "They'll send it through the canal. Drive it in by truck from there. Then there's the pass. Eight weeks maybe?"

"That long for something as simple as love?"

I swallowed and nodded, felt her press against my shoulder as I turned in my chair. "How much should I order?" I picked up a pencil and a requisition tablet.

Her eyes narrowed in thought. "I don't know."

"Well, is it a small space or a large space?"

She looked confused. "Pardon?"

"The space," I said, "where you need the love?"

"Oh. I don't know. Is it important?"

I nodded. "It is. Too much love in a small space, it'd drive you mad."

"Why is that?" she asked.

"I think it's because love rapidly expands, depleting the oxygen and eradicating all life but its own."

"But oh," she said, "what sweet madness it would be." She pursed her lips. "Eight weeks? It took me three to get here."

"Damned elevators," I said. "But you don't need to go back. You can stay here with me. I have an extra cot in the back office."

Clip-clap, clip-clap across the tile. Heat receded as she paced away. She laughed. "You're a troll," she said. "Why ever would I *stay* here with you?"

She had a point. I *was* a troll. Of sorts. Supplies or bridges, it matters little. Trolls guard. I thought about my donut. I thought about the love leashed somewhere behind me. I thought about the girl in red *everything* pacing the sub-sub-basement clerk's station at the foot of the storeroom doors, three weeks down the stairs and ladders of the Bureaucracy.

I grimaced. "I don't *know* why you'd

The Doom of Love in Small Spaces

stay here with me."

I snuck a glance at her. Creamy white thigh peeking out, smooth curves, legs scissoring. I stood up and lumbered toward the phone on the wall. I lifted the receiver and held it to my ear, ringing the crank. "Gallingwise Seven Six Three, please," I told the operator when I heard her cut in.

When Central Stores picked up, I read off the requisition numbers, ordering an abstract by numeric coding. They gave me release order numbers that I scribbled in blue pencil onto the requisition forms.

I tore off the sheets and gave her the carbon copies. "Eight weeks, they said, give or take. You're still welcome to stay. I've got running water, too." I sat back down at my desk, chair groaning beneath my weight.

Her eyebrows lifted. "Running water? Hot or cold?"

I smiled. "Both."

She tossed her hair again and struck a pose. "Do you have any idea how hard it is to get *this* look out of a bucket of secondhand washwater?" Or rusty water from a broken pipe, I thought. I'd watched her through my periscope that morning before she tackled the last half mile or so of her journey down, before I knew I was her destination.

I could have her, I thought. I could have her here for eight weeks with me only it wouldn't be because of me. It would be because of the makeshift tub, the series of pipes and tubes and hoses tapping into the central boiler. Little comforts I'd rigged to make my job more tolerable. But the *because* didn't matter.

"It's that bad up there, is it?" Of course, I knew that it was.

She rolled her eyes. "Fifth floor is a wreck. Frankly, none of the others between here and there are all that wonderful, either."

"But I'll bet the seventh floor is just fine." Of course, I also knew *this*. That was the Board's floor and I kept it that way just as I kept the other floors the way *they* were. Memos flying from my pen. Keep the Machine under a constant state of stress

The Doom of Love in Small Spaces

and alarm, taut with opportunities for improvement . . . just like the world beyond our little game of government.

"Have you ever been to the seventh floor?" she asked.

"Wouldn't want to," I said. "Incompetent gits, the lot of them."

A moment of fear washed her face and she blushed at it. She looked around slowly. "I can't believe you *said* that."

"Why? It's not as if they can hear." And, I told myself, it's not as if it weren't true. They *were* incompetent. That's why they needed me.

She paced some more. "Running water and a cot?"

"And donuts," I said, "Delivered every Tuesday." I paused. "I might even have some extra liquid hand soap lying about. Makes a passable bubble bath."

Her smile shown out not just from her face but from every part of her, beaming out from the tips of her fingers and the ends of her hair and the curves of her hips and breasts, the line of her legs and neck, the exhilaration of her eyes.

"I'll stay," she said.

"I'll call up to five and let them know."

"No need," she said. "The phones are out past the third floor."

"That's unfortunate," I said. But of course, I'm the one who kept them out. "I'll send up a memo then." I grabbed a memo form and rummaged through the box near my desk for an undented pneumatic carrier. "It'll take longer, though."

She curtsied. "Thank you, kind sir." Her brow furrowed. "I don't believe we've been properly introduced. I'm Harmony Sheffleton," she said, extending her hand.

I shook it. Her hand disappeared in my own massive fist. "Drum Farrelley."

"Drum as in Drummond?" she asked.

I nodded. "Glad to know you." And I tried not to smile, tried not to show her that I was as excited about her staying as she was, though for different reasons. But I failed. I felt my fat lips twitch into a grin. "Let's get you that bath," I told her.

And that was how we met.

The Doom of Love in Small Spaces   93

TIME MOVED AT MEASURED PACE AS it does in all Bureaucracies. And here, in the tangled, loose ends of the Great Red-Tape Wrap-Up, there was really not much work to do anymore. Inventory and a bit of paperwork, filing and a bit of maintenance. Few came for supplies these days and I liked it that way. It gave me time to admire my guest.

Her first bath set the tempo for our time together. It quickly became a daily ritual for her to lay in the tub up to her neck in warm bubbles while I sat on the other side of the cracked door. We kept the door between us and we talked. Mostly about work but sometimes about life because the two were so intricately intertwined.

"My job is dull beyond measure, utterly uninteresting," she said during her third bath. "But yours is quite fascinating. Tell me more, Drum?"

And I did.

Our first week slipped past. On Tuesday, the Rationer came with his donuts, unlabelled tin cans and packets of instant coffee. He even had a few mealy apples that I swapped a case of obsolete toner cartridges for. Harmony clapped her hands with delight when I showed her, then suddenly because serious as she lowered her voice.

"Won't you get in trouble for that?" she asked.

"For *what*?"

"Those toner cartridges—" she started.

"Were completely worthless and taking up valuable and much-needed storage space," I finished for her. "Just part of the job."

She raised one of the apples to her mouth. I watched her lips part, watched her shiny white teeth slide into the pockmarked red skin. It's my heart, I thought. She's biting into my heart and in seven weeks there won't even be a core to show it was ever there. The tube whistled and groaned, a battered carrier dropped into the cradle.

Harmony stepped towards it, setting

the apples on my desk. "May I?"

I nodded.

She opened the carrier, pulled out the memo, unfolded it, read it. I watched her eyes move back and forth, her lips now tightly pressed together. She looked up. "They'll expect me back with the love once it arrives. Until then, I should make myself useful to you down here."

She crumpled the memo and moved towards the furnace.

"We usually file all correspondence," I said as she tossed it in.

"Sorry. I didn't think it was important."

"It probably isn't," I said.

She grinned. "So after my bath, I'll make myself useful to you." She picked up the apples, stepped closer to me. My size dwarfed her.

"Any good?" I asked.

She smiled and stepped even closer, now eclipsed by the shadow of me. I could smell Grundy's Liquid Anti-Bacterial Hand Soap rising from her skin in waves but it could've been summer sun on a field of roses. I could see the swell of her breasts as they struggled to fit a bra two sizes too small, the white skin disappearing into a trace of red lace. She lifted the apple, the meat glistening where her teeth torn into its skin. The apple rose slowly and I watched her wrist, her fingers, her arm as they traveled upwards towards me with it. She held it under my nose, near my snaggle-toothed mouth.

"Taste and see," she said.

AFTER HER BATH, SHE HUNG HER clean clothes on the makeshift line by the boiler. I had rummaged an oversized jumpsuit from the janitorial supplies. She held the collar closed with one hand while she slung her clean dress, bra and panties over the makeshift line with the other. My own clothes from yesterday still hung there and I blushed when I saw her dainty scraps of underwear next to my tent-sized, tattered and stained boxers.

Four weeks had passed now. She'd

taken twenty-nine baths. I'd sat outside the door each time, listening to the music of her movement in the water, listening to the wet slap of cloth on concrete on the days that she scrubbed her clothes.

"So what are we doing *today?*" she asked.

"Inventory, I think."

Her eyes lit up. "Can we do the abstracts this time?"

I thought about the love I'd hidden there and the small box of second-hand hope concealed behind row upon row of ennui, terror, despair and longing. I shook my head. "No, it's paper today."

She pouted. "But *I* want to do the abstracts."

I remembered the time I dropped a bottle of despair, splattering my boots with thick, black strands. I'd had to burn them eventually. "Trust me," I said. "You really don't."

"I *want* to do the *abstracts*." She stomped her foot. Then, her mock anger collapsed on itself and she burst into a fit of giggles.

I chuckled at her. She offered a sheepish grin.

"Paper it is," she said.

The front office bell chimed and we went out, hoping it was the Rationer. He'd not shown up Tuesday for the first time in seventeen years.

Now he stood in the office, bruised and bandaged, on a Thursday.

"Black Drawlers on the stairs," he said, patting his sword. We made our trades. He threw in an extra can of potted meat as an apology and I threw in an extra box of Number 1 Pencils as a thank you. Keeping the Machine broken was one thing; Drawlers in the stairwells was another.

Harmony's eyes had gone wide. "Black Drawlers? Here?"

"Sometimes," the Rationer said as he hefted his pack into a battered wheelbarrow. "It's the season for them."

I looked at the calendar and flipped the page. He was right. After he left, his wagon wheels squealing on the tile, I looked up at her. "It *is* the season," I told her, dropping my fat finger onto the day after tomorrow.

Her eyes danced. Music thrummed from her muscles as they followed her eyes, dragging her body into a little jig.

"Do you celebrate down here?"

"Not usually. You?"

She shook her head. "We used to. I miss it."

So the next day, we made our little red hats from cotton swabs and construction paper and paste. She opened eight unlabeled cans, mixed the fruits with fruits and the vegetables with the potted meat and two fistfuls of rice. I took a screwdriver to the furnace grate and pushed the office's single faux-leather couch in front of it. We wore our hats and ate our rice stew while watching the fire sort itself out.

"Do you have a copy of the Cycle?" she asked between spoonfuls. "My mom used to read it to me every Dragon's Mass Eve."

"I know it by heart," I said.

Her eyes widened. "Drum, you surprise me. What's a troll like you doing with scripture rattling about in his head?"

I set my empty bowl on the small table between my massive feet. "I wanted to be a priest when I was younger. Spent a year in the seminary, then gave it up for all of this." I swept my arm wide to encompass our surroundings. I barked out a laugh. "My own kingdom."

She looked around. "It's a bit small." Her forehead wrinkled. "Why didn't you stay on with the seminary?"

"The world wasn't in a good place for it. Civil service seemed a better bet. Of course, this was thirty years ago. When I was closer to *your* age."

"I'm older than I look," she said. She wriggled herself closer to me. I looked down at her, inhaled the scent of her hair and skin. She put her bowl down, lay back and closed her eyes. She still radiated more heat than the fire but a month of life with her and I didn't have to worry about catching fire anymore. The deepest places in me had burned to the ground on that first day. "Will you recite it for me?" she asked.

"I haven't said it for a long time," I said.

"You'll do fine." She opened her eyes, trapped me in them briefly, then closed them again. "Please?"

I cleared my voice. "Muscles tire," I said, my voice rumbling low into the room. "Words fail." I paused to let the language set its own pace. "Faith fades." I watched her, watched her own lips moving to the words as mine did. "Fear falls." Her eyelids twitched a little. She was watching me watch her and a smile pulled at her mouth. I paused again, then closed my own eyes and gave myself to language and mythology. "In the Sixteenth Year of the Sixteen Princes the world came to an end when the dragon's back gave out . . ."

I recited it all the way through. Afterwards, we didn't speak. Together, we lit a candle for the broken dragon upon whose back the world languishes. Then, we turned towards the north, knelt on the floor with my hands swallowing hers, and whispered a prayer for the Santaman's second coming.

Later, we ate our fruit salad and talked.

"Do you believe in the Santaman?"

Harmony asked between bitefuls.

I shook my head. "Not really. I did once."

"I don't think I do, either. If he were real, he'd have come back by now."

"Maybe," I said, "he's waiting for us to figure things out for ourselves."

"Or maybe our hearts are too small for that kind of love," she said. "Like you were saying when we first met: The doom of love in small spaces. Maybe if he *were* to come back now, we'd go insane from it. Maybe this broken world is opening us up somehow, making us really, really ready for him."

"I like that," I said. It reminded me of my job. Keep the Machine in disrepair and disconnect, keep the thousands of us in the Bureaucracy inches from disaster to bring out our best and finest effort. I smiled down at her. "It has a certain poetry to it."

She bit her lip. A devilish light sparked in her eyes. "Are you ready for your gift?"

"A gift? You got me a gift?"

She nodded. "It's Dragon's Mass Eve,

The Doom of Love in Small Spaces

Drum. Of course I did. You can't celebrate Dragon's Mass without gifts."

I sighed. "I didn't get you anything. I just . . . didn't think about it." But of course I had. I'd thought about it ever since the Rationer reminded me of the day. For something like thirty years, the only things I'd ever let loose from my supply room had been the scant little I had to in order to keep my job. Except for the seventh floor, but I told myself that was just to keep the Board greased up and pliant. Still, I'd walked the aisles of my lair looking for something, anything, to give the girl in red. I'd even taken down the small box of hope, shaken a bit into my big hand, before tipping it carefully back inside.

Harmony stretched herself up on the couch. "Well, I have an idea about that," she said.

"What's that?"

She drew her face closer to mine. I could smell pear syrup on her breath; it intoxicated me. "I'll give you my gift. And if you like it, you can give it back to me."

I frowned. "Shouldn't it be the other way around? If I *don't* like it, I give it back to you?"

She shook her head. Her hair flowed like liquid midnight when she did. "It's what *I* said."

"Okay. If I like it, I can give it back."

She pulled away, her face concerned. "Are you sure?"

"Yes."

She leaned back in.

Then she kissed me.

And because I liked it, I kissed her back.

At seven weeks, the phone rang when she was in the bath.

"I'll get it," I said.

After the call, I went back to my place by the door.

"Who was it?" she asked over the noise of the water.

I rubbed my face. I planned a lie,

planned it well, then failed miserably to deliver it. "It was Central Stores," I said. "There's a bit of a problem."

"What's that? Truck break down?"

Worse, I wanted to say. Our world is out of love, it's on backorder. They sent the ship but the ship sank on a reef and the world's last love drowned in the hold. But suddenly I couldn't speak. Suddenly pin-pricks pushed at my eyes and darkness dragged at my heart. I thought about my secret stash and knew that soon I'd have to tell the truth. But for now, after a lifetime of success disappointing others, I didn't have it in me to disappoint her. "Nothing important," I said. "They're just running a bit behind. I'll send up another memo and let them know."

The door opened. She stood there in nothing but a towel that hid little. "How far behind?"

"A few more weeks."

"I'd like that," she said. "Besides, I still haven't helped you with the abstracts." She turned, poised on the tips of her toes, her dark hair plastered over her upper back and shoulders.

"Trust me," I told her. "They're pretty much the same as everything else." I snorted. "You've picked the rest of it up quite quickly. You could probably *do* this job when I retire."

She flinched; I should've wondered why.

"You're retiring?" She used the heel of her foot to push the door partly closed. From the corner of my eye, I saw brief flash as the towel dropped to the floor.

"Someday," I said. "Don't know what they'll do without me." But I *did* know. At least, I thought I did before Harmony walked into my office looking for love. Before meeting her, I'd known the place would fall entirely once I stepped down. I'd kept the Board distanced from the rest of the Bureaucracy. I'd sent them the cream and others the curds. I'd kept the Machine barely functioning but once I moved aside, our small space in the world would collapse in on itself. The other six floors would storm the seventh in a rage. But now I wondered. Maybe someone else could take my place, could prolong the inevitable until the world's groan wound its way north. And maybe—though I doubted it—maybe in the north, salvation would stir and a red-clad myth would strap on his sword, saddle up his wolf-stallion and ride south to find us and show us a new home.

My sudden collision with truth and passion unsettled me.

"What are you going to do?" She asked. Now I could hear her scrubbing her clothes. "When you retire, I mean?"

"I used have it all planned out," I said. "I was going to cash in my pension and buy a horse. Ride west."

"Why not now?" she asked.

"Epiphany," I said.

"No, *Harmony*," she answered. "I'm Harmony."

"No," I said. "I *had* an epiphany."

She laughed. "That's my sister's name. So when did you have this epiphany?"

A minute ago, I didn't say. "Doesn't matter."

The door opened. She stood in front of me, freshly scrubbed, wearing the oversized jumpsuit. She hadn't kissed me since Dragon's Mass Eve. And I hadn't tried to kiss her. But once in awhile, in the midst of our days, there would be a pause, a moment where we simply stood still and looked at one another.

We had our moment and then we went to work.

On the morning of the seventh day of our eighth week, she skipped her bath and wore her red dress instead of the coveralls.

"It's time for the truth, Drum," she told me, "no matter how hard it is."

She'd caught me. I didn't know how. Maybe she'd read it on my face all this time. I'd lived by lying my entire life but somehow she saw past it and knew me. I put my head in my hands.

"I'm sorry, Harmony," I said.

She looked surprised. "What are you sorry about?"

"That call from Central Stores last week. The shipment isn't running a few weeks late."

"Drum, that's not important."

"No," I said. "You're right. It's time for the truth. There's no love coming. There's none to send. The ship went down, all hands lost." I paused. More truth pushed at me. "But that's not all," I said.

Her eyes blazed at me. "I didn't come here for the love, Drummond."

And suddenly, I realized what she meant about it being time for the truth. Time for *her* truth, not mine. Time to uncover *her* lie and lay it out for me to see.

"I'm not even from the fifth floor." She waited. The fierceness in her eyes abated, became a smolder then ashes mixed with rain. "I'm from the seventh."

I growled. It started in my belly and worked its way into my throat and past bared teeth. "You lied to me. You're from the Board, aren't you?"

She nodded, her eyes wandered to the clock. "The memo should be here any minute." The rain drowned the ashes. Her lip quivered and she started to cry. Her shoulders shook.

I wanted to grab her and shake her, toss her about like the toy she made me feel like. "All that interest in my work? All that *making yourself useful?*"

She nodded. "I'm your replacement." She looked up, her face glistening from tears and snot. "When they ran the ad, I applied for it. I wanted to make things better. *They* wanted to make things better, too."

The pneumatic tube clanked and groaned. A heavy carrier dropped into the cradle.

I turned away from it. I opened the carrier and a battered gold watch fell out, far too small for my thick wrist. A card fell out, too.

I ripped it open and read the message. Gratitude of the Board and all that rubbish. Warmest wishes for a happy retirement. Utmost confidence in Miss Sheffleton's capabilities.

I looked over at her. Her dress rippled with her sobs.

She saw me looking. "I don't want it anymore, Drum."

I didn't say anything. I turned around and left.

She found me sitting in the back of the storeroom. I sat on the floor, stroking love's soft underbelly. It rolled its eyes at me and tried to lick its lips behind the muzzle.

I'd decided it wasn't so bad after all. I'd given my thirty years. I'd even decided that her betrayal was a blessing in disguise, jarring me out of a rut I'd lain in for too long.

I felt her hand on my shoulder. "Will you ride west?" she asked.

I shook my head. "I don't know."

"Stay with me," she said. "Don't retire. We can work it together." She waited. When I didn't answer, she added: "I want you to stay."

I scratched behind love's ears. "Would we keep things the same or let them fall apart?"

"Neither," she said. "We'd make them better. It's time to try a new way."

She knelt down, her own hands petting the love. It twisted to get more of her. "What's this?" she asked.

More truth, I thought. "It's love," I said. "I lied before about being out. I just wanted you to stay here with me." I looked at her. "I was tired of being alone."

"Imagine it," she said. "You and me. We fix the elevator and the phones, first. Get the supply chain running so that Facilities can take over the repairs. Before you know it, we'd have a different world."

"And," I said, "we'd have some love and a little hope."

She grinned. "You've got hope here, too?"

I smiled. "Only a little."

She kissed me for the second time. I kissed her back.

"Okay?" she asked.

The Doom of Love in Small Spaces   113

"Okay," I answered.

I felt along love's muzzle and found its buckles with my fingers.

Harmony reached over and slipped love from its leash.

AFTERWORD & ACKNOWLEDGEMENT:
On Flakes of Hope and Litters of Love

M*USCLES TIRE. WORDS FAIL. FAITH FADES. Fear falls.*

As is often the case with my writing, I had no idea what I was starting when I put down those words back in Fall 2004, writing what I thought was an exercise that turned into my shortest story ever, "The Santaman Cycle," and a sale to Jay Lake's first solo editing project, *TEL: Stories*.

And then nearly a year later, in Fall 2005, I set out to write a spicy slipstream story for another of his projects and found myself creating The Bureaucracy and its basement supply troll, Drum Farrelly in "The Doom of Love in Small Spaces." And midway into drafting that story, I discovered that "The Santaman Cycle" was actually the scripture and creation mythos of that odd, new world of mine that involved flakes of hope and muzzled love.

Afterword & Acknowledgement 115

And then we leap ahead six years to Fall 2011, when Tor.com invited me to write their holiday story while I was processing what it meant to lose my parents and become a parent in the span of the same eighteen months. And right in the middle of drafting Mel Sheffleton-Farrelly's story of loss and love, my father-in-law died suddenly and the story became even more timely as I watched my wife at the time face that loss while parenting our twin daughters.

This is one of those stories that says a great deal about what is important to me and how I see life. It captures my journey through losing my parents and discovering the continent of love that becoming a parent opened up to me. And at the same time, it speaks to my former faith and my transition as a Baptist minister to a secular progressive. If we have favorite Story Children, this is one of mine.

And then we leap forward to another autumn as I sit and write this in September 2019. A lot has changed since 2011. There was the crescendo of my big tussle with PTSD and my five Chicago Blocks thanks to Dr. Lipov. There were more losses: My stepmom, Jay, the marriage. And then moving a few times and returning to work as it became clear my writing career wasn't going to be even close to sufficient. There was a lot of putting one foot in front of the other in a dark place until I struck hope. Or, as Melody says, hope struck me.

It came in the realization of how powerful it is to live front and center, in this moment, rather than sliding off into the past or future. A simple truth that I had no understanding of in my PTSD-riddled former life where memory and imagination keep you out of the Now. But I fell into the moment in 2016 and the profundity of it has made a tremendous impact on my well being to the point that I've put fiction largely on hold while researching the non-fiction project that has organically grown out that experience. I've piled up stacks of books and watched or listened to thousands of hours of scientists, philosophers and psychologists in the last three years, slowly distilling down what has changed my life so completely into a simple book.

I was well into this research last Fall when I went on a date and ended up talking about the book I was trying to write and what I'd learned. The woman's face lit up, and when we had our second date, she brought me two books that quickly became core bits of new research. Learning to live in the Now with another person over this last year has been a powerful time for me, so I've dedicated the print version of this story to Amber. Thank you for bringing your own awareness to my newest project and to my life. The now we find together is mighty and I am grateful for you.

And that starts off my thank you's. There are more.

Thanks to John Pitts for insisting "The Santaman Cycle" was a story that Jay needed to see.

Thanks to Jay Lake for agreeing and putting it into print. And for wanting a spicy slipstream story even though Doom wasn't what you were looking for. Because it lets me say ...

Thanks to Shawna McCarty for running "The Doom of Love in Small Spaces" in *Realms of Fantasy*.

Thanks to Patrick Nielsen Hayden for asking me to write a holiday story for Tor.

com and to Greg Manchess for the stunning Santaman art.

Thanks to Lizzy and Rae for being the ground of home and hope, my growing little litter of love.

Thanks to Patrick Swenson for putting this into print with Fairwood Press, and thanks to his son, Orion Swenson, for his amazing cover.

Thanks to Tina Connolly for her beautiful introduction and for bringing Mel to life with her performance on the *Journey Into . . .* podcast site, which you can all listen to here:

http://journeyintopodcast.blogspot.com/2016/12/journey-141-if-dragons-mass-eve-be-cold.html

Last but certainly not least, thank you for buying another one of my books. I am grateful.

Ho, ho, ho!

Ken Scholes
Cornelius OR
September 2019

ABOUT THE AUTHOR

Ken Scholes is the award-winning, critically-acclaimed author of five novels and over fifty short stories. His work has appeared in print for nearly twenty years. His series, *The Psalms of Isaak*, is published by Tor Books and his short fiction has been collected in three volumes published by Fairwood Press. Ken is a winner of the Writers of the Future Award, France's Prix Imaginales, the Endeavour Award and a scattering of others. His work is published internationally in eight languages. Ken's also a public advocate for people living with C-PTSD and speaks openly about his experiences with it. Ken is also a performing musician, presenter and consultant. A native of the Pacific Northwest, he makes his home in Cornelius, Oregon, where he lives with his twin daughters. Learn more about Ken and his writing at www.kenscholes.com.

OTHER TITLES IN THE NOVELETTE SERIES
from Fairwood Press:

The Specific Gravity of Grief
by Jay Lake
small paperback: $8.99
ISBN: 978-1-933846-57-6

Welcome to Hell
by Tom PIccirilli
small paperback: $8.00
ISBN: 978-1-933846-83-5

Mingus Fingers
by David Sandner & Jacob Weisman
small paperback: $8.00
ISBN: 978-1-933846-87-3

Slightly Ruby
by Patrick Swenson
small paperback: $8.00
ISBN: 978-1-933846-64-4

ALSO FROM
Fairwood Press:

All Worlds are Real: Short Fictions
by Susan Palwick
trade paper $17.99
ISBN: 978-1-933846-84-2

The Arcana of Maps and Oher Stories
by Jessica Reisman
trade paper $17.99
ISBN: 978-1-933846-91-0

Truer Love and Other Lies
by Edd Vick
trade paper $17.99
978-1-933846-85-9

The City and the Cygnets
by Michael Bishop
trade paper $19.99
ISBN: 978-1-933846-78-1

The Girls With Kaleidoscope Eyes
by Howard V. Hendrix
trade paper $17.99
ISBN: 978-1-933846-77-4

Street
by Jack Cady
trade paper $17.99
ISBN: 978-1-933846-90-3

The End of All Our Exploring
by F Brett Cox
trade paper: $17.99
ISBN: 978-1-933846-71-2

The Sacerdotal Owl
by Michael Bishop
trade paper: $17.99
ISBN: 978-1-933846-72-9

*Seven Wonders of a
Once and Future World*
by Caroline M. Yoachim
trade paper: $17.99
ISBN: 978-1-933846-55-2

Paranormal Bromance
by Carrie Vaughn
Signed & numbered hardcover: $35.00
ISBN: 978-1-933846-73-6

On the Eyeball Floor
by Tina Connolly
trade paper: $17.99
ISBN: 978-1-933846-56-9

80+ More Titles Available at:
www.fairwoodpress.com

CPSIA information can be obtained
at www.ICGtesting.com
Printed in the USA
JSHW020911151119
2454JS00001B/3

9 781933 846866